# "Here I Am!"
## said Smedley

First published in Great Britain 2000 by Mammoth
an imprint of Egmont Children's Books Limited
239 Kensington High Street, London W8 6SA.
Published in hardback by Heinemann Library,
a division of Reed Educational and Professional Publishing Limited
by arrangement with Egmont Children's Books Limited.
Text copyright © Simon Puttock 2000
Illustrations © Martin Chatterton 2000
The author and illustrator have asserted their moral rights.
Paperback ISBN 0 7497 4240 2
Hardback ISBN 0 431 06981 6
10 9 8 7 6 5 4 3 2 1
A CIP catalogue record for this title is available from the British Library.
Printed in Dubai.

# "Here I Am!"
## said Smedley

by Simon Puttock

illustrated by Martin and Ann Chatterton

**Blue Bananas**

For Andrew

S.P.


For Sophie and Danny

M.C.

Smedley was a very shy chameleon.

He was so shy that he blended right into

the background. Wherever he was, he sort

of disappeared. He just couldn't help it.

At home, Smedley became part of the furniture. His mum and dad could never find him when they wanted him.

'Here I am!' said Smedley.

At school, he blended in so well, nobody noticed him.

'Where's Smedley?' people said.

'Here I am,' said Smedley, but quietly, because he was so shy. He never joined in. He just BLENDED in.

Then one day, there was a new girl in class. Her name was Sally Skinky, and she was bold and bright. She wore purple spectacles and bright green hair ribbons. No one could help noticing Sally Skinky.

'You can sit next to Smedley,' said the teacher. 'At least, I think that's you isn't it, Smedley?' she added, peering hard.

Smedley was busy blending in.

The big girls' gang, who sat in the back
row, giggled.

Smedley blended in a bit more.

'Hallo,' said Sally Skinky.

'Are you talking to me?' asked Smedley.

'Who else?' said Sally, wiggling her eyebrows so that her spectacles joggled up and down. 'The invisible man?'

'Oh,' said Smedley shyly. 'Hallo.'

She's . . . sort of nice

At break time, Sally hung out with Smedley. He felt a bit nervous standing next to someone so NOTICEABLE.

'Hey, new kid, who are you talking to?'
asked the big girls.

'I'm talking to my talented friend,
Smedley,' said Sally Skinky.

The big girls ran away giggling.

Talented! Smedley blushed right into the

brickwork. 'Excuse me,' he said softly,

'but why am I talented?'

'WHY ARE YOU TALENTED?' cried

Sally Skinky.

'Gosh golly, Smedley! You are the
completest camouflager, the best
blender-inner I have ever seen.
A talent like yours could go far.'

'Oh,' said Smedley softly. He had never
thought of going far before.

'Of course,' said Sally Skinky, 'blending in isn't everything. There are lots of other things you could do with a talent like yours.'

'Why,' she exclaimed, pointing to a poster, 'I bet you could even win first prize in the Big City Art Exhibition.'

The Big City Art Exhibition! The BIG
prize! Wow! but –

'I couldn't do THAT!' said Smedley,
alarmed. 'What if I WON? Everyone
would LOOK at me!'

'Exactly,' said Sally Skinky, 'and
EVERYONE would see how talented
you are.'

Smedley was not convinced. 'Anyway,' he shrugged, 'I'm no good at pictures.'

'NO GOOD AT PICTURES?' yelled Sally Skinky. 'Just what do you think you do all day?'

'Smedley, you ARE pictures. Lots of pictures. You can make yourself look like anything you want!'

'I can?' asked Smedley, surprised.

'Of course you can. As a matter of FACT, you could really stand out.'

'Oh no,' said Smedley shyly, 'I could never do that.'

But a small voice inside Smedley wondered, would it be SO bad to be noticed? Secretly, he started practising at home in front of his bedroom mirror.

First, he tried being just one colour all over.

Soon he could do stripes

and spots.

Then one night, he became a bunch of flowers. 'Wow!' said Smedley. He had to admit, it was pretty good. But could he EVER do it in front of other people?

At last, he plucked up his courage and shyly told Sally Skinky what he was doing. 'That's GREAT,' said Sally. 'Why don't you show me?'

'Impossible!' said Smedley. But inside, a small voice said, 'Could I? Maybe?'

In class, he passed Sally a note. It had one word on it. The word was 'LOOK.' Sally looked.

Smedley took a deep breath for courage and held out his hand.

There in the middle of his palm, was a beautiful flower. Then it wobbled shyly and faded away.

Sally wrote Smedley a note back. It said
'SUPER DOOPER DOUBLE WOW
FANTASTIC!'

After that, Smedley practised harder than
ever. Sally helped. She was his audience.
She was very encouraging.

On the morning of the Big City Art
Exhibition, Sally KNEW Smedley was
ready.

'Do you REALLY think I can do it?'
asked Smedley shyly.

'No doubt about it,' said Sally. 'Easy
peasy.'

The Big City Art Exhibition was to take place at six o'clock. Everyone with a picture lined up for a number. Smedley lined up too.

'Where's your picture?' asked the woman at the desk.

'It's a surprise,' said Smedley softly, and he went to stand in the space that had his number next to it.

I CAN do it . . . I think.

At six o'clock, Smedley steeled himself.
'You can do it,' said that small voice
inside him. And right there, in front of
hundreds of people . . .

Smedley

stopped

blending

in.

Then he started standing out. Bit by bit,

he became a tropical sunset,

a wild and jazzy pattern,

an ocean wave,

and, last of all, a beautiful bunch of flowers.

'Here I am!' said the voice inside

Smedley, 'HERE I AM!' it shouted.

EVERYBODY noticed Smedley, and EVERYBODY cheered, even the big girls' gang.

'Bravo, Smedley,' Sally Skinky shouted, 'bravo!'

Of course Smedley won first prize. A newspaper photographer took a picture of Smedley standing beside his number.

Oh dear. Smedley wasn't sure about THAT!

Afterwards, Sally walked Smedley home.

Smedley was very quiet.

'Aren't you glad you did it, Smedley?'

asked Sally.

'Erm . . . ' said Smedley.

'You were GREAT!' said Sally.

'Erm . . .' said Smedley.

'In fact, you're the BEST!' said Sally.

'Erm . . .' said Smedley.

When they got to Smedley's house,
Smedley had a special present waiting
for Sally.

'These are for you,' he said quickly,
giving Sally a big bunch of beautiful
flowers. 'To say thank you.'

'Thank YOU,' said Sally. 'It's an honour to have such an amazingly talented friend.'

Smedley, who was blending in for all he was worth, went pink with pleasure all over.

'And it's an honour,' he said shyly,

'to have YOU for a friend.'

'Oh!' said Sally turning pink too.

'Erm . . .' she wiggled her spectacles up
and down.

Smedley waited, but Sally didn't say
another word.

She was feeling shy.

Of course, Smedley still blends in sometimes. And sometimes, he is OUTSTANDING.

# BLue Bananas

Don't forget there's a whole bunch of
Blue Bananas to choose from: